MILO'S HAT TRICK
STORY AND PICTURES BY JON AGEE

MICHAEL DI CAPUA BOOKS • HYPERION BOOKS FOR CHILDREN

FOR AUDREY

Designed by Alison Donalty   First edition, 2001   Third printing, 2002

He was called Milo the Magnificent. But Milo wasn't
magnificent at all. He botched his card trick. He tangled
his rope trick. And his hat trick was just pathetic.

Mr. Popovich, the theater manager, was furious. "Milo!" he barked. "I'll give you one more chance. Tomorrow night you better pull a rabbit out of your hat—or else."

So the next morning, Milo went out to catch a rabbit.

Instead, he caught a bear.

"What are you doing out here?" said the bear.

"Uh, I'm looking for a rabbit . . . for my hat trick."

"Hat trick?" said the bear. "Maybe I can help."

"You?" said Milo.

"Watch this," said the bear.

And he jumped into Milo's hat.

"Wow!" said Milo. "How did you do that?"

"Easy," said the bear. "You just pretend your bones are made of rubber. It's a secret I learned from a rabbit."

"You definitely can help me out," said Milo. "But you'll have to hide in my hat until we're on stage."

"No problem," said the bear. "Just whistle and I'll pop out."

On the train back to the city, Milo was in a daze. "It's true!" he thought. "I really do have a bear in my hat!"

But when he got to his dressing room, his hat was empty. Worse yet—it wasn't even his hat!

Milo raced back to the train station. There were lots of people with hats, but none of the hats was his.

Meanwhile, in a restaurant across town, someone whistled for a waiter.

"TA-DA!"

Right on cue, the bear popped out of the hat. But there was no applause.

There was no Milo!

"Uh-oh," said the bear. He grabbed Milo's hat and ran.

"Help!" cried a cab driver. "A wild bear is on the loose!"

"A bear? Where?" said a policeman.

"He was standing right by that mailbox. Then—poof!— he disappeared."

"Oh, gosh!" said the bear. "How in the world will I ever find that magician?"

Just then a lady was passing the mailbox. "Hurry up, children!" she said. "Or we'll be late for the magic show!"

"Magic show?" thought the bear. He slipped out the slot and quickly joined the line.

Minutes before the matinee, Milo slouched into the theater. "It's no use, Mr. Popovich," he said. "I didn't find a rabbit."

"Rabbit or no rabbit, you've got to go on," Mr. Popovich said. "Just look, the house is packed!"

Milo looked. A very familiar hat was sitting in the front row.

"My hat! Would you please hand me my hat?"

Milo whistled and out popped the bear.
"Boy," said the bear, "am I glad to see you!"

For the rest of the afternoon, the bear jumped in
and out of hats of all shapes and sizes.
Milo's new act was a smash!

Mr. Popovich was ecstatic. For three solid weeks,
Milo and the bear were the hottest ticket in town.

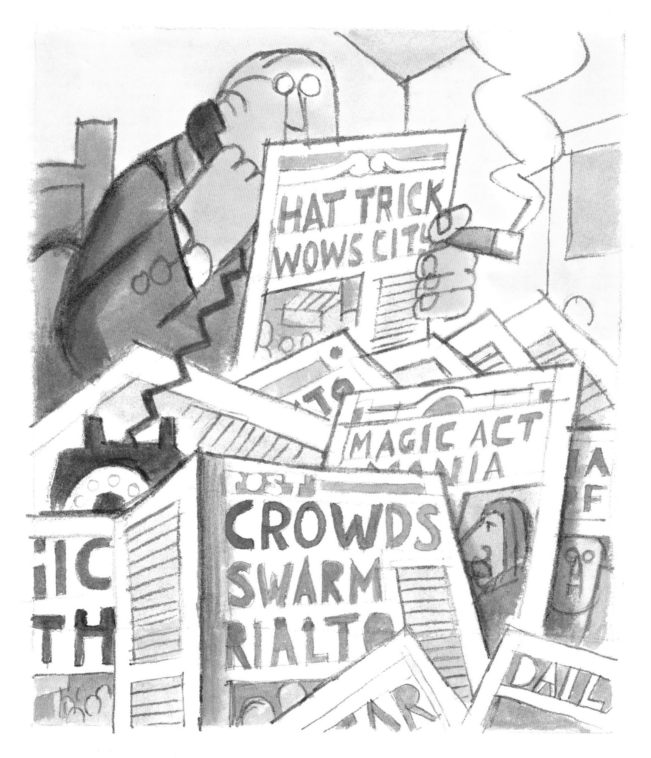

But one day, during intermission, the bear yawned
an enormous yawn. After popping in and out of seven
hundred and sixty-two hats, he was pooped.

So Milo took the bear home.

Back in his cave, the bear settled down for a long nap.

"Gee," said Milo, "what am I going to do without you?"

The bear yawned. "Like I said before, you just . . ."

And then he was asleep.

These days, Milo closes his show
with a hat trick.
And this one is really special.

It's a secret he learned from a bear.